Like Dirt

Abby felt like she had been dunked in ice-cold water. Her hands and feet were numb. All eyes were turned on her. She wanted Mama.

"What gave you the idea you could come in here?" the manager asked.

"A man . . . a man in a monkey suit gave me this." She held out the flyer. Her hand was shaking. "I figured it meant it was okay for me—"

"Probably picked it up off the floor!" interrupted another customer in line.

Suddenly, the man in the monkey suit was coming up the escalator.

"There! He's the one," she said, pointing. "Ask him." Abby's voice was shaking. "He gave it to me."

The manager hurried over to him and whispered something. The monkey-man took off his mask. He was about the same age as her cousin John. Only he was white. He smiled at Abby.

"Sure," he said. "I gave her a flyer." He didn't sound Southern.

Abby was relieved. But the manager gave the young man a nasty look. "You made a mistake, a big mistake," she told him. "Don't you know better than that?"

OTHER BOOKS YOU MAY ENJOY

Amos Fortune, *Free Man*	Elizabeth Yates
Bird	Angela Johnson

Boys of Wartime:
    Daniel at the Siege
    of Boston, 1776
	Laurie Calkhoven

Boys of Wartime:
    Will at the Battle
    of Gettysburg, 1863
	Laurie Calkhoven

The Brooklyn Nine	Alan Gratz
Brown Girl Dreaming	Jacqueline Woodson
The Real Lucky Charm	Charisse K. Richardson
The Real Slam Dunk	Charisse K. Richardson
Roll of Thunder, *Hear My Cry*	Mildred D. Taylor
Saint Louis Armstrong *Beach*	Brenda Woods
Scraps of Time: *Away West*	Patricia C. McKissack
Scraps of Time: *The Home-Run King*	Patricia C. McKissack
Scraps of Time: *A Song for Harlem*	Patricia C. McKissack

SCRAPS OF TIME

Abby Takes a Stand

1960

by

PATRICIA C. McKISSACK

illustrated by

GORDON C. JAMES

PUFFIN BOOKS

PUFFIN BOOKS
An imprint of Penguin Random House LLC
375 Hudson Street
New York, New York 10014

First published in the United States of America by Viking,
a division of Penguin Young Readers Group, 2005
Published by Puffin Books, a division of Penguin Young Readers Group, 2006

Text copyright © 2005 by Patricia C. McKissack
Illustrations copyright © 2005 by Gordon C. James

THE LIBRARY OF CONGRESS HAS CATALOGED THE VIKING EDITION AS FOLLOWS:
McKissack, Patricia C., 1944–
Abby takes a stand / by Patricia C. McKissack ; illustrator Gordon C. James.
p. cm.
Summary: Gee recalls for her grandchildren what happened in 1960 in Nashville,
Tennessee, when she, aged ten, passed out flyers while her cousin and other adults
held sit-ins at restaurants and lunch counters to protest segregation.
ISBN 0-670-06011-9 (hc)
[1. Segregation—Fiction. 2. Civil rights demonstrations—Fiction.
3. African Americans—Fiction. 4. Nashville (Tenn.)—Race relations—Fiction.
5. Tennessee—History—20th century—Fiction.] I. James, Gordon C., ill. II. Title.
PZ7.M478693Ab 2005
2004021641

Puffin Books ISBN 9780142406878

Printed in the United States of America
Book design by Nancy Brennan

27 29 30 28

To Mark Fredrick, the newest McKissack to share
with his cousins, Peter, James, and John-John

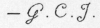

I dedicate this book to my wife, Ingrid, and to our
baby daughter who will have joined our family by
the time this book is published. You ladies are my
motivation and inspiration. I also dedicate this
book to my parents, Thomas and Beatrice James,
who gave me pride and confidence and continue
to support me in all my endeavors.

Contents

In Gee's Attic 1

CHAPTER 1 5

CHAPTER 2 13

CHAPTER 3 19

CHAPTER 4 25

CHAPTER 5 33

CHAPTER 6 43

CHAPTER 7 51

CHAPTER 8 57

CHAPTER 9 65

CHAPTER 10 69

CHAPTER 11 79

CHAPTER 12 85

Another Scrap of Time 95

TIMELINE 100

In Gee's Attic

The "way back place" was what Mattie Rae called the attic in Gee's big white house. It was where her grandmother kept shoes, books, furniture, army medals and trophies, boxes full of clothes, and cartons of old toys. There was all kinds of stuff that once belonged to people in their family who had lived way back a long time ago. Most of them had died before Mattie Rae or her cousins, Aggie and Trey, were born.

"Everything up here is a part of the past. They are all scraps of time," Gee told them as she switched on the light. Then she turned on the ceiling fan to get the air moving. "I want you all to help make a scrapbook."

The attic smelled old with a hint of mothballs. Aggie loved the smell, but it made Trey sneeze. He had allergies.

"This whole attic is like a big scrapbook," said Aggie.

Mattie Rae spotted a menu. It was shiny plastic and decorated with little monkeys swinging from hoops. She picked it up. Across the top in fun lettering was the name THE MONKEY BAR. "This looks like a good scrap," she said.

Gee laughed. "Funny you picked up that old menu. It's from a restaurant that was in Nashville, Tennessee."

"That's where you lived once, right?" Trey asked.

"Yes. That's right. The restaurant closed years ago. But in nineteen sixty, it was the place children wanted to go, especially if you were ten years old like a girl named Abby."

"That's your name," said Aggie.

Gee closed her eyes and sighed.

Chapter 1

Best Friends

"Quick, Mr. Ford. What's the date today?" Abby asked.

Mr. Ford looked surprised, but he checked a calendar tacked to the wall above the cash register. "February second, nineteen sixty."

On cue, Abby and her best friend Patsy slapped each other's hands. Then they clapped twice, snapped their fingers three times, and touched elbows. "What's happening?" they asked together. "You've got it," they answered, pointing to each other, then burst out laughing.

Mr. Ford laughed, too, and shook his head.

He had seen this routine before. This was the girls' special greeting. What he didn't know was why.

Abby and Patsy had made it up after sitting through the sci-fi thriller *Invasion of the Body Snatchers* four times.

"I'll know if an alien takes over your body if we add a move that only the two of us know about," Patsy had said. "On odd-numbered days, we'll snap our fingers two times," she suggested. "And on even-numbered days we'll snap three times."

"Yes! That'll trick an alien," said Abby. It was their secret. So far nobody had figured it out.

Patsy was the *best* best friend. She loved scary movies and she knew how to keep a secret. Nothing was more fun than trading comic books, riding their bicycles, eating dill pickles

with candy canes stuck in the middle, and, of course, just about everything else.

"How will I last two weeks without you, girl?" Abby asked.

They had met at Mr. Ford's for a farewell milk shake. Patsy's grandmother, who lived in Washington, D.C., had been sick. Patsy's family was going to stay with her for a while.

"I am going to miss you soooo much," Abby added.

Patsy was busy buying school supplies to take to Washington. Her mama was a teacher, and she was making sure Patsy stayed on top of her lessons.

"Girl, you've got to see the red-and-white pencils over there. They look like candy canes," Patsy said.

"I knew you'd like those pencils," Mr. Ford

said, chuckling. "Red and white being your school colors and all." He went back to stacking canned goods.

Patsy picked out pens, paper, and a package of the special red-and-white pencils. Then she turned to Abby. "I don't think they're here."

Abby knew exactly what Patsy was looking for. A Big Blue Notebook. They'd seen it advertised in the last issue of *Teen* magazine.

The Big Blue binder was extra large with pockets for loose papers in the front and back. It came with five dividers with plastic tabs in bright colors, one for each subject. But what made it special was its bright blue cloth cover. It was perfect and would make them stand out from the other girls in fifth grade. They'd each saved money to buy one.

Mr. Ford looked around his shop. There were

items on shelves and tables from floor to ceiling. He sold everything from groceries to jewelry and from hand-packed ice cream to fresh fish. He had so much crammed in his small shop, it was hard to find anything. But if you asked, Mr. Ford generally knew where everything was.

"Ummm," he said, thinking. "I'm not sure if I have any blue binders, but I do have black and red ones for sure."

The girls already had black binders. They knew what they wanted. Nothing else would do.

Patsy's eyes brightened. "Hey, maybe I can find a Big Blue while I'm at Granny's house."

Abby didn't have any relatives who lived out of town. All of her family lived in Nashville. Aunt Mitty—Mama's sister—Uncle Big John, and her favorite cousin, John, lived next door. Although he was eighteen years old and in college, Abby liked being around John. He was like a big brother.

After Patsy paid for their supplies, the girls flopped down on one of the two stools at the small counter.

"A strawberry shake, please," Abby said to Mr. Ford.

"Promise to write?" asked Patsy.

"Why? Nothing exciting ever goes on around here."

They watched Mr. Ford make the shake. He never rushed to do anything. Slowly he took the vanilla ice cream out of the freezer. Then he dug out three scoops and added six plump fresh strawberries. After adding a bit of milk, he zapped the mixture in the blender and poured it into two big glasses. The shake was so thick and creamy Abby always ate hers with a spoon.

As they were leaving, Mr. Ford called to Abby, "Tell me the name of that notebook again."

"Big Blue. It's the latest. It's the greatest!" Abby shouted.

Chapter 2

The Monkey Bar Grill

"Mama," Abby asked as she helped dry the dinner dishes, "may I go to town with you tomorrow? They have Big Blue Notebooks at Harveys. I have just enough of Grandma Turner's birthday money left to buy one."

"I suppose," Mama answered, rinsing the big cast-iron skillet that she had used to fry chicken. Then, with two hands, Abby placed the heavy skillet on the stove where it would wait to fry bacon for breakfast the next morning.

"Ever thought about getting a new skillet?"

asked Abby. "This one is so old and heavy."

"Nope." Water swished out of the drain as Mama emptied the dishpan. "New isn't always better," she said. "That old skillet knows how to cook."

"And it fries the best chicken in the world," said Abby. She folded the dish towel and placed it on the rack.

The next morning, Abby was up early. She put on her navy blue suit. Mama tied up her hair with a matching blue ribbon.

"I want to get to town and back before it gets too crowded," said Mama.

Mama slipped on her patent leather shoes and placed a lavender hat on her head. After she picked up her gloves and purse, the two of them put on coats and hurried to catch the 9:15 bus.

Abby and Mama sat right up in front. There

was no need to go to the back of the bus any longer. It was 1960. Black people could sit wherever they wanted on public buses. But in many ways blacks and whites were as separated as ever. Abby and Patsy still attended an all-black school. Folks couldn't get certain jobs. Nobody could live in a white neighborhood. Theaters, hotels, amusement parks, and restaurants all over town had awful signs. WHITES ONLY. All except for the Nashville Public Library. Abby and Patsy went there often.

Although the day was cold, it was sunny. As the bus rolled past Tennessee State University, Abby could see the track team practicing.

The bus eased its way down Jefferson Street where the black stores were. Abby looked at the window display of the Lord and Lady Dress Shop. Mama had bought the suit she was wearing there last Christmas. Next, the bus moved past Otey's Grocery Store, where she and Patsy got dill pickles, and the Cameo Restaurant. It served the best chili in Tennessee. They passed the back of Fisk University's Jubilee Resident Hall and the Ritz Theatre, where she and Patsy had seen the *Body Snatchers* movie. As the bus went by Ford's Variety Shop, Abby waved at Mr. Ford, who was sweeping the sidewalk in front of his store. He waved back.

At Eighth and Jefferson the bus turned, and Abby saw shoppers at the farmers' market. Farther away the State Capitol building sat high atop a mound.

Abby held Mama's hand as they walked from the bus stop to Harveys. Abby turned her head so she wouldn't have to see the WHITES ONLY signs in the window of Hi-Style Hair Salon and Southland Restaurant. Abby understood why Mama never lingered downtown. She always finished her business and caught the next bus home. But today, Abby wasn't going to let anything ruin her shopping. She was going to Harveys to get her Big Blue Notebook.

Chapter 3

Turned Away

At Harveys Department Store, Mama went to make an exchange. "Meet me at the front door in thirty minutes," Mama called over her shoulder. "And behave," she added.

Harveys was a big, fancy department store. There was so much to see that Abby's eyes never knew what to settle on first. The ground floor was laid out in a circle. The up and down escalators were located in the center. Abby loved the mirrored ceiling over the cosmetic counters. It made her dizzy to walk and look up at the same time. The bright lights made even the costume jewelry sparkle like real gems. The real jewels were displayed in a cabinet lined in black velvet. Abby imagined herself wearing one of the diamond necklaces with earrings to match.

When Abby passed the perfume aisle, her nose tingled from the various scents. She sneezed and thought about how much Patsy enjoyed testing perfume samples. From luggage Abby passed through pocketbooks and shoes. Then suddenly, between scarves and gloves, a giant monkey leaped in front of Abby, startling her.

"Come ride the merry-go-round and have lunch at the brand new Monkey Bar Grill on the third floor," he said, bowing.

"Thanks," Abby said to the person in the monkey costume. She smiled and accepted the flyer.

She read some of the menu items on the flyer. "Lion Burgers, Savannah Fries, and Kilimanjaro Shakes—made with three scoops of creamy strawberry ice cream, capped with a mound of rich whipped cream and topped with a fresh strawberry—nineteen cents."

The flyer had a coupon for a free ride on the merry-go-round. Abby had never been on a merry-go-round. And this one was indoors. Abby quickly added up her money. She had enough to buy a Big Blue *and* have a strawberry shake. Abby glanced at the clock over the elevators. There was even enough time for a ride on the merry-go-round.

But what if there was a sign at the Monkey Bar? A sign like at the other restaurants downtown? But the man in the monkey costume had given her a flyer. He wouldn't have done that if she weren't welcome. Right? She headed for the third floor.

Yellow cardboard monkey paw prints were glued to the floor. The paw prints led her to the Monkey Bar Grill. Brightly colored stools in shades of orange, lime green, and lemon yellow circled the counter. A fake leopard-skin canopy hung over it.

Abby's eyes went straight to the merry-go-round. Children rode up and down on lions, elephants, crocodiles, monkeys, and tigers. Abby chuckled to herself. Whoever had designed the merry-go-round didn't know much about Africa. There were no tigers there. She'd learned that in kindergarten.

Abby took her place in the line at the Monkey Bar. It was crowded and noisy. Kids pushed and shoved. Some were laughing while others were crying. Mothers scolded their children or let them scream. A few of the children looked at Abby as if *she* belonged in a zoo.

Then all at once a woman standing behind Abby snapped crossly, "What are *you* doing in line?" Her voice was as sharp as a needle.

Now a young woman in front of Abby turned around. "Well! Of all the nerve! I'll tell you something right now. . . . If *she* stays, I'm leaving!"

An older lady with three small children started shouting, "Where's the manager? We need the manager over here!"

Suddenly, a big woman in glasses that looked like cat's eyes came rushing over. "I'm the manager," she said. "And I assure everyone, *she* is *not* staying!"

Chapter 4

Like Dirt

Abby felt like she had been dunked in ice-cold water. Her hands and feet were numb. All eyes were turned on her. She wanted Mama.

"What gave you the idea you could come in here?" the manager asked.

"A man . . . a man in a monkey suit gave me this." She held out the flyer. Her hand was shaking. "I figured that meant it was okay for me—"

"Probably picked it up off the floor!" interrupted another customer in line.

Suddenly, the man in the monkey suit was coming up the escalator.

"There! He's the one," she said, pointing. "Ask him." Abby's voice was shaking. "He gave it to me."

The manager hurried over to him and whispered something. The monkey-man took off his mask. He was about the same age as her cousin John. Only he was white. He smiled at Abby.

"Sure," he said. "I gave her a flyer." He didn't sound Southern.

Abby was relieved. But the manager gave the young man a nasty look. "You made a mistake, a big mistake," she told him. "Don't you know better than that?"

Abby was surprised when the young man answered, "Oh! I'm sorry. A New Jersey fellow like me just isn't used to these rules. And you're right. I *did* make a mistake. Taking this job was a mistake." He took off his costume, shoved it at the big woman, and walked away.

Turning, the manager pointed her finger at Abby. "He's not from around here!" she snapped. "You are! And you know we don't serve Negroes in here. Have you forgotten your place?"

Suddenly it was quiet. Even the children had stopped crying. Abby's stomach churned and her legs felt like rubber bands. Tears stung the corners of her eyes, but she refused to cry. "I'm sorry. I'll leave," she said.

"No need to worry," the manager told the customers. "She's going!" She waved her arms at Abby as if shooing away a pesky gnat. "Go back to enjoying yourselves, everybody."

Somehow Abby's feet got her to the front door of Harveys. Mama was waiting there.

"What's the matter?" Mama asked. "No note-book? Don't worry. Maybe we can find what you're looking for at Woolworth's."

"I want to go home," Abby said, fighting back tears. "Now!"

Abby waited until she was on the bus before telling Mama the whole story. "It made me feel like . . ." Abby searched for a word to describe her feelings.

"Like dirt," Mama said. "Like nothing but a piece of dirt. I know, honey. I know."

Abby nodded, unable to speak. Finally she said, "I didn't know I was doing wrong."

"No!" Mama sounded angry. She lifted Abby's chin. "No shame on you! You didn't do anything wrong. The wrong was done to you!"

The bus stopped to pick up more passengers. At Tenth and Jefferson, her cousin John hopped up the steps. He took the seat in front of them.

"Hello, Aunt Bea." Then he turned to Abby. "Hey Peat," he said with a big smile. "Where's Repeat?" He called her and Patsy "Peat" and "Repeat," because they were always together.

"Patsy's at her grandmama's," answered Abby. She kept her head down so he couldn't see her red eyes.

"You're awfully quiet," John said.

Abby shrugged.

During the ride home, Mama told John what had happened at Harveys.

"That's why I want you to come tonight," he said, turning to Mama.

He told them there was going to be a meeting at the First Baptist Church at seven o'clock. "We're planning to protest," he said. "We won't accept the way we're treated any longer—we won't! But we need people to help."

Abby had never heard her cousin talk this way before.

"Can we count on you to come, Aunt Bea?"

"Protest. . . ." Mama sounded uncertain. Then she touched Abby's arm. "I'll be there."

Abby was surprised. Mama had never gone to a protest meeting before.

"Me, too!" Abby said. "Mama, if you're going to be a protester, I am, too!"

Chapter 5

Meeting Time

By six thirty P.M., the First Baptist Church was so crowded, people had to stand outside in the churchyard.

Abby's third-grade teacher was there. So were the school custodian, and her dentist. She waved at Mr. Ford and Mama's beautician, Miss Alfreda. She wished Patsy were here with her. It was exciting. A real protest meeting.

The only people she didn't see were Uncle Big John and Aunt Mitty, John's parents.

"Shouldn't we save them seats?" Abby asked.

"No," said Mama. "I don't think they'll be here."

Abby wanted to ask why, but the meeting was beginning.

There were a few announcements, and then Reverend Kelly Miller Smith, the pastor of First Baptist spoke first.

"Good evening, everyone," he said in a powerful voice that filled the room. "Some of you folks are attending a meeting like this for the first time. We say, 'Welcome.' We're here tonight to talk about freedom. But freedom is a meaningless word when we Negroes don't have the same rights as white people." The reverend looked around the church. "Are we free to live in any neighborhood we want? . . . No!"

His voice grew louder now. "Are we free to work where we want? . . . No!

"Are our children free to attend better schools?" he asked.

This time people shouted, "No!" along with Reverend Smith.

"Are we even free to buy a cup of coffee and sit down to drink it where we please?" he asked, his voice rising with emotion.

Now there was a thundering chorus. "No!"

Reverend Smith shook his head. "No. No, we're not. America is supposed to be a democracy where we are all equal. But segregation says we're not. Democracy and segregation are like oil and water. The two don't mix."

People clapped and shouted "Amen." Mama was as still as a stone, listening to every word.

"If we don't stand up for ourselves, who will?" asked the pastor of another church.

For about an hour, different speakers, many

of them preachers from the neighborhood, talked about how segregation hurt everybody and needed to end. *Had* to end.

Mr. Ford stood up and spoke to the crowd. "I'm sixty-four years old. I know what's wrong with segregation. Tell me what can we do to change it?"

There were cheers, amens, and applause.

John stood up next. "For the past few days, some college students over in Greensboro, North Carolina, have been staging a sit-in at the lunch counter of Woolworth's," he said. "And we're getting ready to have our own sit-ins, right here in Nashville."

Then suddenly, Mama stood up, too.

Abby could tell Mama was nervous, because she turned her ring around and around on her

finger. And her pocketbook was clutched tightly under her arm while she spoke.

"Henry and I wanted things to be better for Abby, our daughter."

Abby was surprised. Mama hardly ever talked about Daddy. He'd been killed three years ago in a railroad accident.

"I still hold on to the dreams we shared for her. But that's not easy to do here in the South."

Mama paused. The room was silent. Mama began speaking again. Now her voice was steady. "Just today, my child was turned away from a new restaurant at Harveys. So I've made up my mind. If she can't have a sandwich there, I won't buy our clothing there. I will not spend a dime in a place that humiliates my child! Never again. No more!"

Mama sat down. She held Abby's hand. Mama was shaking. People leaped to their feet. "That's right! No more. No more!" they chanted. Abby couldn't believe it. Mama was a protester!

The meeting ended soon after. John rushed over to Mama. "Aunt Bea, you were something. I wish you'd talk to MaDear. My mama doesn't think protesting will make a bit of difference. She says I'm wasting my time."

"I thought that way myself. And you know your mother. She is hard to convince," said Mama. "But I'll give it a try."

While Mama stepped away to chat with a church member, Abby stayed with John. She wanted to ask why Aunt Mitty didn't believe in protests. But John was talking with two girls his age.

"We want to start sit-ins," he said. "But we have to train everybody. We'll teach you exactly what to do . . . and what *not* to do. We can fit you in around your classes. Please sign up. We need your help."

"What's a sit-in?" Abby asked.

"We go in a group and sit at a lunch counter," John told her. "The waitress probably won't serve us, because we're Negroes. But we won't just get up and leave. We'll sit at the counter all day, until it closes. Then we'll go back the next day and the next, until they serve us."

"Sure. I'll do it. I'll sign up," said one of the girls. She was tall and pretty, with ruler-straight teeth and bright brown eyes.

"You have to be eighteen," said John.

"We both are," she answered. "I'm Teri and

this is my roomie Joan. We're at Tennessee State. Count us both in."

"How'll I reach you?" John asked.

"You can reach me—I mean us—" Teri said, smiling, "at Hale Hall. So like I said, count us in . . . for the sit-ins. . . . Let us know . . . what to do . . . you know."

John was still smiling as the girls walked away.

"She sure is cute," said Abby. "I bet that's why you wanted her to sign up."

John laughed. "Oh, Peat, being cute's got nothing to do with this. Sit-ins are serious business. People may get hurt. It's not as simple as it sounds."

Abby blew air through her teeth. "Okay, Mr. Smart Guy, how many sit-ins have you been in?" she asked, knowing the answer.

"None," John said, shrugging, but added quickly, "But I've been through the training. I know what nonviolent protesting means. I'm ready."

John seemed different lately. More serious.

"It's not fair. I want to do something, too," Abby insisted.

"Don't worry," said John. "You will!"

Chapter 6

<hr>

Protest

Dear Patsy,

Sorry I haven't written sooner, but I've been busy.

Guess what? I'm a civil rights activist! Today I helped John get people signed up for sit-ins at downtown lunch counters. You have to be eighteen. But I'm part of the Flyer Brigade. We pass out flyers telling people about meetings and protests. The flyers tell people about nonviolent protesting. No matter what, the people at sit-ins can't strike back. John has been through the training. Now he's training others.

I wish you were here. I feel like I'm part of something big! Gotta go now. Hope your grandmama's feeling better. I'll write later.

Your bestest friend in the whole wide world,
Abby

On Saturday morning Abby went back to the First Baptist Church with Mama and Mrs. Leona Whiteside. But no Aunt Mitty.

"Negroes have no money, no power, and no protection. How can we win against odds like that?" Aunt Mitty had asked Mama.

"David took out Goliath with five smooth stones and a slingshot," Mama had answered.

Aunt Mitty was not convinced.

In the church kitchen, Mama tied on her apron. She had her big cast-iron skillet with her. The ladies were cooking up more food than Abby had ever seen. Word was five hundred students had gone out in groups to sit-in at Woolworth's, Kress's, and McClellan's. Other stores, too. They were all dressed in their best Sunday clothes.

"It's all so crazy when you think about it,"

Mama said, snapping beans. "Those young people will spend hours sitting at a lunch counter and come back here hungry!"

Mrs. Whiteside shook her head and clicked her teeth. "Segregation comes up short any way you cut it."

By the time the first protesters came back from their two-hour shifts, Mama and the ladies had fried chicken ready.

"We just sat there at the counter," said a boy in a Fisk University T-shirt. "We didn't get served. But neither did any of the white people waiting for a seat and yelling at us!"

By mid-afternoon, word came that the Harveys manager had closed the store early.

Abby felt hopeful. "We won! We won! If they stay closed, they'll go out of business!"

"Honey, you don't think it's going to be that easy? No way," said Mama.

Abby understood what Mama meant when she saw the evening news. Aunt Mitty came by to return Mama's pinking shears just as the Harveys manager was on television. She sat on the couch with Mama and Abby.

"I don't believe most colored people agree with what went on here today," said the manager. He went on to say the protesters were just a few troublemakers trying to ruin it for all the good colored folks of Nashville. Aunt Mitty looked nervous and worried.

"Don't y'all fret none." The manager looked into the camera and pointed his finger. "We will not let a bunch of riff-raff come in our store and stop us from serving our customers. We'll be open for business in the morning and things will be as usual. You can count on that."

"Why didn't they give our side?" Abby complained. "It's not fair!"

"That's what I've been trying to tell my stubborn son. Life is not fair," said Aunt Mitty. "Segregation is the way it's always been. John is headed for nothing but trouble trying to change things. You'll see. But he won't listen to me or his father. Maybe he'll listen to you, Bea. Will you talk to John?"

Mama shook her head. "No, Mitty. I won't," said Mama. "Growing up in the South is like being a bird in a cage. Our children have wings. But they're never allowed to fly. By the time they get to our age, their souls are lifeless. John's mind is made up, same as mine, Mitty. We may not change a thing, but it's worth a try. Don't be afraid. Join us."

Aunt Mitty mumbled something and left in a huff. Before letting herself out the screen door, she called over her shoulder, "Can't say I didn't warn you. This protesting will only bring trouble to our own front door."

Chapter 7

Struggles

"I've never been so scared in my life," said a girl sitting in the church basement. The sit-ins had been going on for about a week. Raw eggs dripped from her clothing. She had been at Woolworth's. "So many people were outside the store, shouting and calling us names."

"Inside, people stood right behind us, throwing things," said the other girl. "We're lucky it was just eggs."

Abby recognized them from the meeting.

She gave them each a cup of the coffee Mama had made. "Did you see John Marshall? Is he okay?"

"Oh, I remember you. You're John's cousin. You were there the day Joan and I signed up." The girl extended her hand, and Abby shook it. "I'm Teri Deets. John and I are good friends now . . . sort of dating . . . kinda." She smiled. "Don't worry. He's okay."

When did John have time to date anybody? Abby thought. She liked Teri. And she liked that John liked her, too. Oh, but Patsy might not be too happy about that. She'd proposed to John when she was three years old.

"Are you going to quit?" Abby asked Teri.

"Never," Teri answered. "I'll be back tomorrow."

All afternoon, Abby helped wherever she

could. She made signs for the demonstrators who marched outside the store. She also made one for Teri to put in her dorm window. On a big piece of cardboard, Abby wrote in red letters:

SAVE OUR NATION
END SEGREGATION

A little later, more students came back. "You should have seen the crowd all around us!" one said. "They called us awful names and told us to go back to Africa." The student shook his head. "I wanted to fight back. I'm afraid next time I will. . . . I can't do this anymore."

Soon John came downstairs, looking exhausted. He was still carrying a sign Abby had made. It said, "Justice for All Americans." There was egg all over it, too.

"Hey Peat," he said, hugging Abby. "We made it through another day."

Then he flopped on one of the cots set up in the church basement. Within minutes he was asleep.

Every night, Abby watched the news on television. The protesters looked so tired. Abby wondered how long the sit-ins were going to last. She wrote Patsy again.

Dear Patsy,

I can't believe it! Nashville is famous, all because of the protests. Mama says the whole world knows what's happening here. Do you see it on TV in Washington?

The protesters sit-in at lunch counters every day. They go to Kress's, Woolworth's, and Harveys.

Lots of angry people show up to yell at them, but they never fight back. John says if they fight back, then the other side wins. Some of the protesters have given up trying. I think John is very brave.

Can't wait to see you.

You are the bestest friend in the whole wide world,

Abby

P.S. John is a team leader. And now I am captain of the Flyer Brigade. Hurry home so you can join us.

P.P.S. John has a girlfriend! Her name is Teri and she is really cute.

Chapter 8

Sacrifices

Abby was out with the Flyer Brigade. Their leaflets read: BOYCOTT SEGREGATED STORES. DON'T SHOP IN STORES THAT DIS- CRIMINATE. Abby handed one to Mrs. Willerby, a neighbor.

"How will I get the things I need if I can't go downtown?" Mrs. Willerby asked.

"I'm not sure," Abby said. "Mama says we'll just make do or do without."

Mrs. Willerby looked at Abby a moment and smiled. "Well, then, I'll do the same."

Mr. Horner took one of the flyers, but he didn't read it. Mrs. Sanders slammed the door after saying, "This is all just a big inconvenience."

"You're just going to bring trouble to us all," said Mrs. Bosley. That was the same thing Aunt Mitty said.

"People like that are just chicken-liver cowards!" Abby told her friends back at her house.

Mama looked at Abby with disappointed eyes. "No, daughter, they are not cowards," she said later. "They are afraid for good reasons. They know what hate groups are capable of doing to black people. We need to be respectful of those who disagree with us. Or we're no better than the mob."

Later that evening, Mama and Abby got ready for a meeting. Next door, Aunt Mitty was taking clothes off the line. Abby went to the fence.

"Come with us, Aunt Mitty. Please, please, please," she said.

Aunt Mitty kept right on working. She didn't answer. Maybe she was thinking about it.

"John is speaking tonight. Don't you want to hear him?" Abby went on.

"Hush, girl!" Aunt Mitty's eyes flashed anger. She tossed a bunch of clothespins in a sack and walked over to the fence. "I'm proud of my son. I love him. And if you loved him, you'd try to stop . . ." Tears were in Aunt Mitty's eyes. And she was unable to finish her sentence.

"Ships are safe in the harbor," said Mama, coming up from behind Abby, "but ships are made for sailing, sister dear."

Abby had heard Mama say that many times.

Now she understood. John was like a ship. He wanted to change things, and that meant he had to go into scary waters.

Mama and Abby went to the meeting at the African Methodist Episcopal Church without Aunt Mitty. It was crowded. Speaker after speaker came up to talk.

"I don't think things will ever change. I've gone to five sit-ins now. We still don't get served. . . . It's awful discouraging," said one man. But right away another man leaped to his feet.

"We must keep the faith," he said. "I for one will not give up until we get what we deserve. Who will stand with me?"

"I will," said Miss Jenkins. She was Mama's friend from the Quilters Society.

"I will," said another person, and then another.

Soon the whole crowd was standing and singing.

It was a song Abby loved, and she sang along, too. "We shall overcome. We shall overcome. We shall overcome somedaaaaay. . . ."

Suddenly, a voice from the back of the room stopped the singing.

"Attention everybody!" a fireman shouted. He was pushing his way to the front of the church. Holding up his hands, he announced, "The meeting's over! According to fire department rules, there are too many of you people in here. Time to go. Now!"

"But, we've never had a problem before," said Reverend Phillips.

"Well, you do now," the fireman said.

"This is just a way to break up our meeting," someone said.

"We won't let this stop us," said another.

"We'll find another place to meet," John stood up and said to the crowd.

Then Reverend Phillips began singing again. A different song, an old Negro spiritual. Abby took Mama's hand and held on tightly as everyone marched out of the church. They sang:

"Ain't gonna let nobody turn me 'roun'
Turn me 'roun'.
Ain't gonna let nobody turn me 'roun'.
I'm gonna wait until my change comes.

Don't let nobody turn you 'roun'
Turn you 'roun'.
Don't let nobody turn you 'roun'.
Wait until your change comes.

I say I'm gonna hold out,
Hold out, hold out.
I say that I'm gonna hold out
Until my change comes.

I promised the Lord that I would hold out,
Hold out.
I promised the Lord that I would hold out.
Wait until my change comes."

Chapter 9

Going Downtown

Dear Abby,

Guess who I saw in a Washington newspaper? John! There he was sitting at the lunch counter. An awful woman was screaming at him. I saved it. Can't wait till I can see it all for myself! Granny's better. We're coming home Saturday. Hooray!

You are the bestest friend in the whole solar system,

Patsy

"Hey, girl," said Abby. It was Saturday morning. "Are you home?"

"Of course I'm home. I'm talking to you, aren't I?" Patsy said, sounding sleepy. "Our train didn't get in until three this morning. All I want to do is sleep. . . ." Patsy stopped talking and pretended she was snoring.

"Wake up! No time to sleep," Abby shouted into the receiver. "There's work to do! The movement needs you!"

"Okay! Okay!" said Patsy. "Later."

Within the hour Patsy was at Abby's house. It was February 27, so they slapped hands, clapped twice, snapped their fingers twice, then touched elbows.

"What's happening?" Abby asked, hugging her friend.

"Well, I'm glad no alien took you over."

"Did you get a Big Blue Notebook in Washington?" asked Abby.

Patsy shook her head. "Naw. Can you believe it? In the nation's capital they'd never even heard of a Big Blue Notebook? I'm still stuck with my old black one, I guess."

"Me, too. When I went to buy a Big Blue at Harveys, this is what happened."

The whole time Abby was telling the story, Patsy held her head down. Her hand was clapped over her mouth.

When Abby finished, Patsy said, "No! You were standing there all alone, with those ugly people staring at you? It makes me so mad. . . . I want to be in a sit-in right now."

"You can't," said Abby. "You have to be eighteen. But we can make signs, pass out fly-ers, stuff envelopes, and help Mama serve the food." Abby could see Patsy didn't think any of that was exciting enough.

Suddenly, a smile spread across her friend's face. "You don't have to be eighteen to *see* a sit-in, right?"

Abby was afraid of what Patsy was thinking. "John says it's dangerous downtown."

"How bad can it be if his girlfriend is there?" Patsy argued.

Abby went to the window. "It looks like it might storm."

Patsy shrugged.

"Our mamas will kill us if they find out," Abby said.

Patsy stood up. "I'm going downtown. Coming or not?"

Chapter 10

Eyewitness

The girls had never ridden their bicycles this far before. Pedaling down Jefferson Street wasn't hard, because it was mostly flat. But it was cold, and the wind was blowing hard. When they reached Eighth Avenue, Abby could see the capitol building sitting on top of an Indian mound.

"Follow Eighth Avenue to Church Street," she called to Patsy. She could hear Patsy panting as they pumped up the steep hill.

"I need to rest and warm up. Let's stop at the library," she said.

They locked their bikes in the library rack. The sky was growing darker and darker.

Mrs. Marcella, a library volunteer, nodded as Abby and Patsy came in the front door. They were regulars who came often.

Abby liked going in the front door. There was no manager wearing cat-eye glasses pointing an accusing finger in her face, telling her to go away. There were no signs telling her to go around to the back door. Here Abby could almost forget about race and prejudice.

Almost. If only there weren't two drinking fountains—one labeled WHITES and the other one COLORED. The one for whites was newer looking. The handle was hard to turn on the one for Negroes. They were separate, Abby thought, but they sure weren't equal.

"I'm warming up some," said Patsy, getting another swallow of water from the colored fountain. "Let's go."

The girls walked straight down Church to Harveys. Right away, Abby sensed something was wrong. The sidewalks were almost empty. She understood why there weren't any black shoppers going in and out of stores. But where were all the white shoppers?

Then they began to hear people shouting and horns honking.

As soon as Abby turned the corner, she saw a huge crowd outside Harveys. Many were teenagers, no older looking than John and his friends. They looked so angry. They were on the sidewalk, in the street, in cars blocking the traffic. Horns blasted.

"They don't like America? They can go back to the jungle!" shouted an angry teenager. "They're not gonna destroy our country!"

"If we lynched a few of 'em, they'd stay in their place!" yelled another.

"Let's teach 'em a lesson," a woman screamed, shaking her fists.

Abby had a sick feeling in her stomach. She grabbed Patsy and ducked into an alley. Patsy's eyes stretched in fear.

"Abby," Patsy whispered, "I-I-I didn't know it was going to be like this."

"Me either," said Abby. She held on to Patsy and didn't move. Was John inside? Maybe his shift was over. Maybe he'd left already.

A moment later, Abby could hear sirens blasting in the distance, growing louder and louder and heading toward them. The girls pressed into the side of the building and peeked around.

"Look," said Abby. "The police are coming."

In the street the crowd parted to allow three police cars through. Policemen jumped out of the cars. They didn't yell at the crowd or tell people to go home. Instead, they rushed into the store. A few minutes later they came back out, dragging protesters, handcuffed like criminals.

Patsy started crying. "I wish we never came!"

"Oh, no! That's Teri," Abby told Patsy, and pointed. "That's John's girlfriend!"

"They're gonna hurt her! They're dragging her like a rag doll!" Patsy covered her eyes.

Behind Teri, Abby saw someone who looked familiar. He was in handcuffs, too. Abby's hand flew to her mouth. "Patsy! That's the guy in the monkey suit! The one from Harveys."

Patsy still wouldn't look, but she said, "White people are in the sit-ins?" She sounded surprised.

"Quite a few," said Abby. Still no sign of John. Maybe he was already back at the church. Eating or taking a nap. Safe.

The crowd grew louder. "Shame on you!" they jeered at the guy from the Monkey Bar.

"Put 'em all in jail and throw away the key!"

Now the police were pushing the protesters into their cars. The lights on top of the police cars started flashing again. The motors revved up.

"Wait," a policeman shouted. "We got one more."

No! It was John!

One officer held him under his arms; another held his legs. People in the crowd called John names. One man kicked John in the side. A woman holding a little boy spit at him. She told her child to spit on him, too.

"*Stop it!*" Abby yelled, and started toward John.

"No!" Patsy said, pulling her back into the alley. "Don't go! You'll get hurt!"

Patsy was right. Abby squeezed her eyes shut as John was thrown into the back of the van.

Just as the protesters were hauled away, the heavens opened. Rain fell in hard, stinging sheets. Lightning flashed. The crowd ran for cover. Abby and Patsy ran back to the library where their bikes were.

"I'm going home. Now!" Abby pushed her foot against the kickstand.

"We can't. Not with the lightning," Patsy said. So they hurried inside.

Patsy and Abby leaned against the smooth marble wall. Patsy took deep breaths to calm herself. She kept saying over and over, "This can't be happening. . . . This can't be happening."

A rush of questions crowded Abby's mind. Why weren't the white teenagers arrested? They were the ones throwing eggs and hurting people! How long would John be in jail? What if the police hurt John? Maybe Aunt Mitty was right.

The rain stopped as quickly as it had started.

"Let's get out of here," Patsy said, heading for the door.

"Not yet," said Abby, turning to the drinking fountains on the opposite wall. She walked over and took a sip from the colored fountain. Then she leaned over and took a big gulp of water from the white one.

Patsy's mouth fell open.

"Now," Abby said, "I'm ready to go."

Chapter 11

Punished

Mama was so angry with Abby she put her on punishment for one week. "No Flyer Brigade. No television. No telephone. And after school, no company. . . . That includes Patsy."

Patsy's mama gave her the same punishment. Although Abby pleaded, Mama didn't budge. "You should have come to me before going to town by yourself," Mama said. "I hate to imagine all the terrible things that might have happened to you."

"If I asked, you would have said no. Besides,

nothing did happen," Abby said. "Not like it did to John."

John had been let out of jail that same evening. He was bruised, and his ribs were sore. But by the next morning he climbed over the fence and came into the kitchen where Mama and Abby were eating pancakes. John joined them.

He was plenty upset with Abby and Patsy. "You're lucky you didn't end up in jail, too," he said. "You should give this hard-headed girl a three-week punishment, Aunt Bea." But he winked when he said it.

"I should," said Mama.

Mama flipped pancakes, while John told them that he and Teri and the others were charged with disturbing the peace, trespassing, inciting a riot, loitering, and a whole lot of other

words that made them sound like criminals.

"What will happen to you?" Abby asked.

"Don't worry. We have people who will help us," he said. "Lawyers. Good lawyers, like Z. Alexander Looby."

John leaned back in his chair. He sighed deeply. "That's not my worst problem. MaDear and Daddy are," he said. "But I am not giving up, not even for them."

"I never want to go near downtown again as long as I live," Patsy said as she and Abby walked home the first day that they were off punishment. They were carrying their same old black notebooks. "That was some scary stuff we saw."

They stopped for a cup of hot chocolate at

Mr. Ford's. Teri and John were sitting at the counter.

"Look who's here. Peat and Repeat," said John.

Abby teased them. "I think *your* names should be Peat and Repeat."

Then it was Patsy's turn. "John," she began in a fake dramatic voice, "I thought we were engaged. But that's okay, Teri. I'll step out of the picture for John's happiness."

John and Teri laughed. They did make a cute couple.

When Mr. Ford saw Patsy and Abby, he rushed over to a box. "They just arrived," he said. A full grin spread across his face. "I looked in every catalog I had, and I finally found your Big Blue Notebooks," he said.

Abby and Patsy looked at each other. So much had happened. The Big Blue didn't seem so important now. But they wouldn't dream of hurting Mr. Ford's feelings. Especially after he had tried so hard to find the notebooks for them.

"Thanks, Mr. Ford. I'll take one," said Abby.

"I'll take one, too," said Patsy.

Mr. Ford smiled. He looked very pleased.

Chapter 12

Victory

The boycotts and sit-ins continued into spring. In April, a house was blown to bits with dynamite. It was the house of Mr. Looby, the lawyer helping the protesters. Luckily, neither he nor his wife were hurt. Right after that, a crowd of students marched to City Hall to see the mayor, Ben West.

Abby and Mama watched it on TV.

"John! I think I see John!" Abby jumped up and pointed at the screen.

He was standing not far from a girl who went right up to the mayor and said, "Mr. Mayor, do you think it's fair that restaurants won't serve people just because of the color of their skin?"

Mayor West looked at all the faces in the large crowd in front of City Hall.

"No," he finally said. "No, I don't."

Mama's hand flew to her heart, as if she couldn't quite believe the words she'd just heard.

But sure enough, one by one the stores began to serve black customers. All except Harveys.

Then finally one Friday evening, John hopped the back fence and came charging into the kitchen. "We won!" John shouted. "Harveys caved in." He picked up Abby and danced her around the table.

Mama smiled through happy tears. Wiping her eye with the corner of her apron, she said to Abby, "And tomorrow, we're going to have lunch at the Monkey Cage!"

"Monkey Bar, Mama," Abby said, laughing. "It's the Monkey Bar."

But later, when she thought about it, Abby wasn't sure about going back to Harveys. She called Patsy.

"Suppose there's a crowd of people waiting to call us names," Abby said.

"This time you'll be with your mama," Patsy answered.

"Come with me?" Abby begged.

"Ummm, not yet," Patsy said slowly. "Maybe another time."

Abby understood how Patsy felt. Part of her

was afraid to go, too. But Mama said, What sense did it make to work hard to change things and then not go when the changes came?

Abby fretted about what to wear. She changed her mind three times. She wanted to look her best. That night, she didn't sleep well.

The next day when they arrived at Harveys, sale signs were everywhere. There didn't seem to be as many customers as usual. And hardly any colored people. But Mama walked to the escalators as though she was on a mission, never lingering to look at a single item.

At the Monkey Bar, Abby was surprised to see that the merry-go-round was gone.

"We took it out," said a waitress as Mama sat on an orange stool at the counter. The waitress poured Mama a cup of coffee. Meanwhile, a man not even sitting near Mama and Abby looked at

them and left before finishing his doughnut and coffee.

"May I have your order?" the waitress said without a smile.

Abby didn't need to see the menu. "A Lion Burger, Savannah Fries, and a Kilimanjaro Shake."

When the food came, Abby ate in silence. It was okay. But the strawberry shake wasn't half as good as the ones at Mr. Ford's. Mama paid for their meal. And they left. Within an hour they were back on the bus headed for home.

So that was it?

Abby looked at Mama smiling to herself. A great big smile! Abby wondered why Mama looked so happy after eating such a dry hamburger.

"One day you'll tell your grandchildren you were the first Negro child to eat at Harveys Monkey Bar," said Mama. Then she handed her one of the Monkey Bar menus. "I want you to keep this. A lot of people—you included—worked hard and sacrificed to make it possible. Don't ever forget that."

"Okay," Abby said, forcing a smile.

Later that afternoon she met Patsy at Mr. Ford's for a real strawberry milk shake.

"After all that?" Patsy said when Abby told her about the Monkey Bar. "You're telling me that the burger was dry and the fries were hard!"

"Right. I thought it was going to be better." Abby remembered what Mama had said. "I don't think the sit-ins were about the food. I think they were about having choices."

"Who would *choose* to pay good money for bad food?" Patsy said.

Abby laughed. "I don't have to eat at the Monkey Bar ever again, if I don't want to. But now it's up to *me*. The choice is mine."

Another Scrap of Time

"Gee, did your friend Patsy ever eat at the Monkey Bar?" Aggie asked her grandmother.

"Yes," said Gee. "She finally went one day with her mama. Then we went together. The food never got any better. When we wanted a good milk shake or a good cup of hot chocolate, we ate at Ford's."

"What happened to John?" asked Trey.

"Oh, John was very active in the movement

all through college and law school. After he and Teri got married, they went down to Mississippi and Louisiana. They helped register people to vote. He became a lawyer and Teri taught high school. They live in Detroit now." She reached down into the trunk. "Here is a picture of them at the March on Washington back in August nineteen sixty-three."

"I know. I know," said Aggie. "That's where Dr. Martin Luther King, Jr., made his 'I Have a Dream' speech."

The children studied the picture closely. "Will they be at the family reunion this summer?"

"I hope so," said Gee. She looked in the trunk for other items from that time. "Then you can ask them what it was like to be at the Lincoln Memorial with all those people—over two hundred and fifty thousand people."

"Did Aunt Mitty and Uncle Big John ever change their minds?" Trey asked.

"Not right away," said Gee, looking in the old trunk. "Look, here is a JFK campaign button."

"What's that?" Trey asked.

"JFK are the initials of John Fitzgerald Kennedy. He ran for president and won in nineteen sixty. He was young and he had a lot of good ideas. A lot of black people liked him and voted for him. They believed he'd help end segregation."

Mattie Rae pinned the button to her blouse. "What did he do?"

"He never really got a chance to do everything he wanted, because he was killed—assassinated—a few months after the March on Washington. November the twenty-second, nineteen sixty-three."

Aggie held up a red-and-white school banner. "This is your high school, right?"

Gee smiled and nodded. "Pearl High School in Nashville. It was still segregated when I went there. Now whites and blacks attend school together all over Nashville, including Pearl-Cohen."

Gee found her old library card, a Tennessee State yearbook, and two ticket stubs from the Paramount Theatre. "I remember when the Paramount first allowed African Americans to come in the front door. Before then we had to use an alley door and go up to the balcony. Black people rarely went downtown to the movies. When Patsy and I bought these tickets, we went in the front door."

"Do you remember the movie?" Aggie asked.

"Sure do. It was *The Magnificent Seven,*

starring Yul Brynner and Steve McQueen."

"Oooooweeee, I like these scraps of time," said Mattie Rae. "Let's put them in our big scrapbook for the family reunion.

"Look what I found," said Trey, holding up a military medal.

Gee smiled. "This is from a long, long time ago. It's something that belonged to my great-grandfather. He fought in the Civil War."

"Will you tell us about him?"

"Yes. I promise to tell you that story the next time we're together."

Remembering How It Was

Although the characters in my story are made up, what happens is real. The places are real, too. There actually was a Harveys Department Store in Nashville, Tennessee, with a lunch counter named the Monkey Bar Grill. Like most restaurants throughout the South, it didn't serve black people. Because of brave protesters, things finally began to change in the spring of 1960. I grew up in Nashville during that time, and I still remember it as if it happened yesterday.

Here's what was happening in 1960.

✦ FEBRUARY 1: Four black students from North Carolina Agricultural and Technical College begin a sit-in at the lunch counter of Woolworth in Greensboro. The sit-in will continue for five months.

✦ FEBRUARY 27: In Nashville, students holding sit-ins in major stores are attacked by white teenagers. The protesters are arrested for disorderly conduct, and eighty-one are convicted and jailed.

✦ MARCH 5: James Lawson, a former graduate student at Vanderbilt University Divinity School in Nashville, is arrested during a meeting at the First Baptist Church. Since 1959, Lawson has been training students to be nonviolent protesters. Just before his arrest, Vanderbilt had expelled him for his involvement in the sit-ins.

✦ MARCH 12: Police use tear gas to break up a black student protest in Tallahassee, Florida. By now, nonviolent sit-ins have spread throughout the country and are often dealt with violently by the police.

✦ MARCH 22: An Associated Press article reports that nationwide, one thousand blacks have been arrested in sit-ins. Both black and white lawyers have volunteered to defend them.

✦ APRIL 19: The home of Z. Alexander Looby, a civil rights lawyer who has been helping the protesters, is bombed in Nashville, Tennessee. More than two thousand students conduct a silent march to City Hall to protest. A student at Fisk University, Diane Nash, confronts Mayor Ben West, asking, "Do you think it is wrong to discriminate against a person solely on the basis of their race or color?" He answers, "Yes."

✦ MAY 10: Six Nashville stores open their lunch counters to black customers, making Nashville the first major Southern city to begin desegregating its public facilities.

✦ JULY 25: The first lunch counter in Greensboro, North Carolina, desegregates.

- ✦ OCTOBER 17: Woolworth, Grant, Kress, and McClellan stores desegregate their lunch counters in 112 cities.

- ✦ NOVEMBER 8: Democrat John F. Kennedy is elected president of the United States. Black voters help him win.

- ✦ NOVEMBER 14: Six-year-old Ruby Bridges is the first and only African-American child to attend an all-white school in New Orleans, Louisiana. Hundreds of white demonstrators protest.

When the year ends, the civil rights movement has won some victories, but the struggle for justice and equality has just begun.

Patricia C. McKissack

The Rules for the Nashville Sit-ins

+ Don't strike back if cursed at or abused.
+ Don't laugh out loud.
+ Don't hold conversations with your fellow workers.
+ Don't leave your seat until your team leader has given you instructions to do so.
+ Don't block entrances to the stores and the aisles.
+ Show yourself courteous and friendly at all times.
+ Sit straight and always face the counter.
+ Report all serious incidents to your team leader.
+ Refer all information (anything that happens to you) to your leader in a polite manner.
+ Remember, love and nonviolence work.

TURN THE PAGE FOR A LOOK AT
THIS FAMILY'S STORY
FROM 1879 —

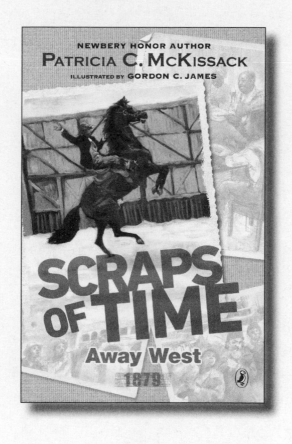

In Gee's Attic

The Webster cousins loved Gee's big attic because there were so many old things in it. Their grandmother called them scraps of time.

Gee kept files of papers and photos, stacks of books, suitcases filled with old clothes, and boxes of toys and games—things that belonged to people in their family. Nearly all of them lived a long time ago. Many had died before Mattie Rae or her older cousins, Aggie and Trey, were born.

They were putting some of the scraps into a

scrapbook to take to the next Turner family reunion.

"The last time we were here," Trey said to Gee, "you promised to tell us about this." He had a box in his lap and was holding up an army medal.

"Whose was it?" Aggie asked.

"It belonged to my great-grandfather, Franklin Turner. He was a Civil War hero. He gave the medal to his son, my grandfather, Everett Turner. Everett's story begins in St. Louis, Missouri," said Gee. "He had just run away from home. It was January of eighteen seventy–nine. He was only thirteen, but he was determined to make it out West."

"Was he scared?" Mattie Rae looked worried. She hugged her stuffed rabbit, Alonzo.

"He should have been plenty scared, but he was too excited," said Gee.

Chapter 1

Stowaway

In the cold darkness, Everett sat squeezed between sacks of sugar, cotton, rice, and tea. All around him he heard mice squeaking and scurrying about. He forced himself not to move or cry out. That old saying about being as quiet as a mouse was dead wrong. He laughed to himself. Mice were really noisy.

Everett was a stowaway. He was hiding in the hold of a supply boat called the *Camel's Back*. It was headed up the Mississippi River to

St. Louis. He'd slipped onboard in Memphis the night before.

Everett's legs ached. He wanted to stand up and stretch, but he couldn't. He might be discovered. Then he'd be thrown overboard. Or worse, he might get sent back to Pearl, Tennessee. And no matter what, he wasn't going home. His future lay in the West.

That's what the handbill said. LAND. OPPORTUNITY. YOUR FUTURE IS IN THE WEST.

All Everett had was twenty-five cents and his pa's army medal. But he was heading west toward his future.

Everett knew he wouldn't have had the nerve to leave home if his brother Cole hadn't gone first. Cole had joined the army. His last letter said he was in Texas, heading for New Mexico. He was a sergeant in the Tenth Cavalry, and had a horse named Jimbo. The Tenth Cavalry was all-black, but all the officers were white. Their job was to keep peace in Indian territory. It was a dangerous job. Everett was proud of Cole.

It was January now. Everett would turn fourteen in July. So he felt older than just thirteen. Still, you had to be eighteen to enlist in the army. Four and a half years was a long time to wait. But he was determined to leave farming behind— *now*! He was sick of crop failures. Why couldn't his oldest brother, Gus, understand that?

"Pa left the farm to us," Gus had said the other night. "We don't have to sharecrop for nobody. We owe it to his memory to make the farm prosper."

Gus wasn't happy when Cole left. But Cole was a "man" and old enough to do as he wished.

So Everett was left stuck on the farm. And no matter how hard they worked the fields, the farm didn't prosper. The land seemed to be cottoned-out. Everett was tired of trying.

"I hate this place!" Everett yelled. "I'm leaving!"

Gus got angry. "Where to? You always jump into things without thinking and end up in trouble. One day I won't be around to help you. What then?"

Everett decided it was time to find out. The next day he ran away, made it to Memphis, and hid in the cargo hold of the *Camel's Back*.

Now, in a few hours, he would be in St. Louis, Missouri. And from there he'd be on his way out West.

He clasped the pouch in his pocket. In it was Pa's medal from fighting in the war. The Civil War.

"You're the only one of my boys born in freedom. And you got the most schooling. It's why I fought in that terrible war. I want *you* to have this," Pa had said not long before he died.

Well, Pa always said being free meant leading the life you wanted. And that was just what Everett aimed to do.

Suddenly, a mouse scampered across his ankle. Its tiny little claws tickled his flesh. This made his leg jump, and he accidentally kicked over a barrel. The barrel knocked over another, and both hit the bottom of the hold with a crash.

"Somebody take a look down there," Everett heard a man say.

There was the sound of running footsteps. The hatch overhead opened. Blinding sunbeams burst through the darkness, shedding light on the cargo bay.

"Captain Brewer, sir!" the crewman shouted, looking down at Everett. "Look at the little mouse I found!"

READ THE NEXT STORY IN
PATRICIA C. MCKISSACK'S
FAMILY SAGA.

For Lilly Belle, 1920s Harlem, "the capital of Black America," is about as far from her hometown of Smyrna, Tennessee, as a twelve-year-old can get—maybe not in miles but certainly in mind-set. A summer program in Harlem for gifted young writers opens a new world for her, where jazz music in the streets lulls her to sleep, her classroom is in a famous mansion called "the Dark Tower," and author Zora Neale Hurston is her teacher. Through a difficult run-in with a sophisticated New York classmate, Lilly Belle comes to a deeper understanding of the power of words, especially her own.

"MCKISSACK WRITES WITH EMPATHY FOR THE CHARACTERS AS WELL AS A GOOD EYE FOR DETAILS THAT BRING THE PERIOD TO LIFE." —BOOKLIST

LOOK FOR ANOTHER PIECE
IN THE QUILT THAT HOLDS
THIS FAMILY'S HISTORY.

Brothers Tank and Jimbo Turner love sneaking into Nashville's Sulphur Dell Ballpark to watch the super-stars of Negro League Baseball. When Josh Gibson, the famous home-run hitter, bunks at their house, the boys think they're one step away from heaven.

"A GOOD CHILD'S-EYE INTRODUCTION
TO BASEBALL'S SEGREGATED PAST."
—*BOOKLIST*